I0685274

Reprint Publishing

FOR PEOPLE WHO GO FOR ORIGINALS.

www.reprintpublishing.com

The Mantel-Piece Minstrels, and Other Stories.

By

John Kendrick Bangs.

New York:
R. H. RUSSELL & SON,
1896.

To Three Little Chaps.

The Mantel-Piece Minstrels.

JIMMIEBOY was sitting in his father's library, the other night, studying the logs that were blazing merrily on the hearth. The flames interested him hugely, rather more so indeed than was usual, because they were apparently excited about something themselves, they crackled and leaped about so strangely. Every now and then, too, it seemed to Jimmieboy as if the crackling sounds he heard were like words, and that the flames were talking about something. At first he could hardly believe that this could be so, but as he crept a little nearer and turned his right ear toward them, as closely as the heat would permit, he was convinced that his impression was the correct one after all. The flames *were* talking together.

"You are not doing it right at all," said the largest flame, with a sputter which one might say was an angry one.

"I'm doing the best I can," said the little blue flame that had been spoken to. "I told you I couldn't dance well when you asked me to join the show. I'm willing to get out if you are not satisfied. I hate minstrel shows anyhow. The only reason I consented to join was that I thought if I became one of the dancing troupe, I wouldn't have to sit out among the audience and listen to the jokes."

"I don't want you to back out," said the big flame more pleasantly. "You are very graceful, but you don't take the right steps. You dance all by yourself instead of with the rest of us, that is all. This is to be a dance in which we all take part, and if it is to be successful we must all work together."

"Well, I just can't," said the little blue flame. "I would if I could, but I can't. When I begin dancing I forget everything else, and I might just as well try to set the river on fire as to keep step with the rest of you."

As the little blue flame said this, Jimmieboy heard a great clapping of hands behind him, and turning to see whence it came, was astonished to see rows and rows of toys seated about him, the dolls grinning as though they wished to make the corners of their mouths meet behind their ears, while all the other playthings, from the fire engines to the glass agates, were chattering away like fine people at the opera and enjoying themselves hugely.

"Why—why where did you come from?" asked Jimmieboy, his eyes getting as large as China alleys, so great was his surprise.

"The question should rather be, how did *you* get here?" retorted the rag-baby,

whom he had addressed. "I didn't know you were to be admitted to our minstrel show. Who gave you a ticket?"

"Nobody," said Jimmieboy. "I just found myself here."

"Well, you'd better not let the ticket-man find you here without a ticket, that's all," said the rag-baby, in a loud whisper. "We're very particular about whom we let in at our entertainments. If the Mantel-Piece Minstrels knew you were here I doubt if they'd crack a single joke or sing a single song."

"But what does this all mean?" queried Jimmieboy.

"It means that this is Fortnightly meeting of the Toy Club, and the Mantel-Piece Minstrels are going to entertain us."

"Who are the Mantel-Piece Minstrels?" asked Jimmieboy.

"Look and see," returned the rag-baby, "and keep still. The performance is about to begin, and if you want to see it you mustn't let it see you."

Jimmieboy looked up as the rag-baby spoke, and what should he see on the mantel-shelf but a long row of pieces of bric-a-brac, blacked up to look like darkies, the clock in the middle looking for all the world like the middleman at the regular minstrels, and at the ends were the grotesque little Chinese god holding clappers in his hands and the dragon-handled Royal Worcester jar holding a tambourine. Between these two were ranged the antique silver match-box Jimmieboy's papa had bought in Italy, the Delft cat, three or four small vases, a sandstone statuette dug up from some old ruined temple in Cyprus, and various other rare objects of art of which Jimmieboy Senior was very fond.

The amazed boy was about to utter an exclamation of surprise when the clock, acting, as I have said, as middleman, began :

" Good evening, Tambo," he said. " I hope I see you well this evening."

" I hopes yo' does," said Tambo. " If yo' eyesight am what she oughter be yo' sees me well enough to obsoyve that I'se as hansom lookin' as ebber."

Here the head of the dragon-handle made a most frightful face, which set all the toys, except the rubber doll, roaring with laughter. The rubber doll squeaked with terror through the whistle between his shoulder blades. It was his first appearance at a minstrel show, and he was afraid the dragon would come down and bite him.

"Put him out!" cried the rag-baby. "Those rubber dolls ought not to be brought to minstrel shows anyhow. They are always squeaking."

"Dat reminds me," said the Delft cat. "I'se got a conundrum. What am de difference 'tween a rubber doll an' a new pair ob shoes?"

"I'm sure I don't know," said the clock, rubbing his hands together. "What is the difference between a rubber doll and a new pair of shoes?"

"I dunno myself," answered the Delft cat. "Dey bofe squeaks so much I nebber kin tell de difference, 'ceptin', perhaps, de pair ob shoes goes on foot an' de rubber doll, he goes on squeakin'."

"Brother Bones will now play on the piano," said the clock, as the toys' laughter over the Delft cat's conundrum ceased.

Here the Chinese god arose and requested one of the fire-engine drivers to go into the parlor and get the piano for him to play on.

"I'se berry sorry for de delay, ladies an' gentlemen," he said, "but I forgot to bring de pianner wid me. I tought I put it in my vest pocket befo' I leff home, but I cyarn' fin' it dere. I must o' put it in my odder clo'es. If any one ob de ladies an' gentlemen happins to hab brought one wid him an' will lend me de loan ob it fo' fibe minutes I'll play on it, an' I promise not to scratch de cover."

"Scratch the cover?" echoed the clock. "Why, pray, should any one scratch the cover of a piano playing on it?"

"Why?" retorted Bones. "Why? Well, it's plain yo' nebber saw a game ob foot-ball."

"Foot-ball?" said the clock. "What on earth are you talking about? What has foot-ball to do with pianos?"

"In dis case it has ebberyting to do wid it," said Bones. "Foot-ball is de only t'ing I kin play on pianners."

"By de way," said Tambo, when the enthusiasm of the audience over this joke had ceased, "our pianner got locked de odder night an' we can't git it open."

"What seems to be the trouble? Can't you unlock it?" asked the clock.

"No, suh," replied Tambo. "All de keys is on de inside."

Here one of the glass agates got hysterical with laughter and the fire-engine had to put him out.

"Well," said the clock, after order had been restored, "Mr. Bones, if you can't play anything but foot-ball on the piano, perhaps there is something else you can do."

"Yassir," said Bones, "yassir. I kin do several things, suh. Ef any one in the audience will give me a mince pie I will perform a little magic wid it."

"Ah," said the clock, "magic, eh? That is good. I am very fond of magic. And what will you do with the pie?"

"I will say one, two, three, and de pie will disappeah, suh. It will disappeah jest like it nebber was, suh."

"That is fine," said the clock.

"Yassir," said Bones, "it will be turned into a minstrel."

"A minstrel!" said the clock.

"Yassir," said Bones, "it will be turned into me. In fac', suh, I agrees to *eat* dat mince pie."

Unfortunately for the hungry Bones no toy in the audience had brought a mince pie along. It was very strange that it should have been so, for, as I have been

informed, most toys when they go to minstrel performances take very good care
before starting out to be provided with
opera glasses to enable them to see the
jokes, fire escapes to enable them to leave
early if they do not enjoy the jokes, and
mince pies to enable them to enjoy the
evening in spite of all adverse circumstan-
ces. So, poor Bones had to forego his
exhibition of magic, but being a minstrel
of much ready wit he covered his disap-
pointment by singing "After the Ball,"
which all the toys vigorously applauded,
not because they liked it, but because the
minstrels didn't charge anything for their
performance, and the "Book of Etiquette
For Playthings" had taught them that
when no pay was required enthusiastic
applause was the proper thing.

" "Dat song reminds me ob a conundrum
I heerd de odder night," put in the ori-
ental match-safe, when Bones had sat
down. "What's de difference atween a
iron dog—one o' dese dogs dey has on
country places to skeer away tramps,
made o' iron an' painted green—an' a fel-

ler what owns a whale whad he wants to sen' to a young lady foh a weddin' presen', but can't put de address on hit, kaze de whale he won't stan' still.''

"Dear me," said the clock, "that is a very long conundrum. I hardly get it through my head. Let me see. One of the things is an iron dog."

"Yassir," assented the match-safe. "A iron dog, painted green ; one o' dem kind whad country people—"

"Yes, I remember that," said the clock, "and the other thing is a whale——"

"Naw, sir. Not a whale, but a *man*

whad *owns* a whale dat he wants to sen'
to a young lady foh a weddin' present,"
said the match safe.

"And he cannot fasten the address on
the whale?" asked the clock.

"Dat's it," said the safe. "Dat's it.
Kaze de whale he won't stan' still. Now,
what am de difference atween dat dog an'
dat man?"

"I knows de answer," said the Delft
cat. "Dey can't either ob 'em bark."

"Dat ain't de answer," returned the
match-safe.

"Hoh!" jeered the Chinese god. "I
knows de answer. De answer is dat you
don't know de answer yo'self."

"Yaas I does, too," retorted the match-
safe. "I knows de answer mighty well."

"Well, I give it up," said the clock.
"What is the answer?"

"All give it up?" put in the match-safe.
The whole row of minstrels nodded
assent.

"Den I'll tell yo'," said the match-
safe. "De dorg—de iron dorg dats
painted green, he has a tail he can't wag;

an' de man wid de whale, he has a whale he can't tag."

"Well, well, well, well!" roared Bones. "Dat is de most tiresomest conumdrum I've heerd yit."

"Yass," said the match-safe. "Dat's why it reminded me ob dat song you sang."

At this the rag-baby got laughing so hilariously that, like the agate, she went into hysterics, and in her hysterics she kicked so hard that her right shoe flew off and struck against the row of chairs in which the marbles were sitting. The force of the blow knocked the marbles off the chair and they fell to the floor with a terrible clatter, which so frightened Jimmieboy that he jumped to his feet and hallooed aloud. Why one of Jimmieboy's halloos, to which all the toys were so used, should have that effect, I certainly do not know, but that it did cause the toys, one and all, to disappear instantly is the truth. Jimmieboy rubbed his eyes in a mystified fashion as he noted the disappearance of the toys, and then

he looked at the mantelpiece to see if the minstrels had also fled. He was relieved to find that they had not done so, but, while they had remained, the show itself was manifestly over, for they had all resumed their natural color and, as far as Jimmieboy could discover, were attending strictly to their regular duties. As for their jokes and songs they have never indulged in anything of the sort since, though several times thereafter the dragon's head on the Worcester jar has looked as if he had something on his mind that he would like to say.

And the little blue flame?

Well, when Jimmieboy looked for him both he and his big dancing teacher were just going out, and so Jimmieboy himself went regretfully up stairs and made ready for bed.

A Lesson in Bird-talk.

A Lesson in Bird-talk.

"IT'S a pity you can't talk," said Jimmieboy, looking at the Robin that was hopping up and down the lawn looking for something nice in the way of a worm to take home to the babies for supper.

"Peep!" retorted the Robin, scornfully, gazing out of one eye at Jimmieboy, its head gracefully cocked to one side. "Pity I can't talk! Ho! humph and pooh! I think it's a pity you can't understand bird language."

Jimmieboy gazed at the bird in aston-

ishment. This was the first time a bird
had ever answered him back, and instead
of wanting his sympathy it absolutely re-
jected it with scorn and completely turned
the tables by pitying him.

"Pity birds can't talk, eh?" repeated
the Robin. "What do you think we're
doing when we say cheep, and week, and
all the other sounds we make with our
throats? Think we're just making a
noise to keep ourselves from falling asleep
on the grass?"

"Are you talking when you make
those chirrups?" asked Jimmieboy, de-
lighted to find a bird who not only could
talk, but was willing to stop worm-hunt-
ing to talk with him.

"Are you talking when you are calling
out 'Hullo-Billy' and 'Howdydotom-
mie' and 'Letsplaytagfellers?'" queried
the Robin.

Jimmieboy laughed.

"Certainly I am," said Jimmieboy.
"But Hullo-Billy and Howdydo Tom-
mie and Lets play tag fellers, all mean
something."

"Well, so do peep and cheep and gur-ryoup," retorted the Robin, "and for my part I think peep and cheep are both better words than letsplaytagfellers, though I can't say gurryoup is an ex-pression I ever cared much for."

"But what does peep mean?" asked Jimmieboy.

"Well, well, well!" chirruped the Robin, tossing its head perkily up and down, and opening its bill as wide as it could, doubtless to laugh. "What does peep mean? Might as well ask your papa what's anything. Why, my dear but highly stupid young man, peep means so many things in our language that it would take me forty-nine years to tell you half of the first third of 'em. It all depends on how many Es there are in it, and at what time of the day we use it, and by whom it is spoken. Plain peep with two Es in it, spoken at 5 o'clock in the morning by a baby robin, means 'good morning, mamma, is breakfast ready?' and her reply using the same word means, 'no, not yet my child, but

it will be shortly. Papa is over in the
new vegetable garden now looking for a
worm ; here is a gnat, and you may have
it if you are very hungry. It will keep
you quiet, I hope, until papa gets back,
for mamma is very tired this morning
and must have a little bit more sleep—
you are getting harder and more muscu-
lar every day, and mamma can't rest as
comfortably on top of you as she could
before you cut your feathers.' "

"My !" cried Jimmieboy. "Does
that one little word mean all that ?"

"That's what I'm telling you," said
the Robin. "Then one hour later at 6
o'clock, that same word 'peep' spoken
by the mother robin, means 'here comes
papa, now, baby, and he's got the finest
angle worm you ever saw for our breakfast ; ' to which the baby answers 'peep,'
meaning 'ain't it bully ; ' and the papa
robin coming in says 'peep,' meaning
'how's that for a morning's work ?' as
he throws the worm into the nest. And
so you see, my boy, it goes on all day.
We find peep a very interesting and use-

ful word. Every day brings some new
meaning to it. For instance, the other
day when you fell down and broke your
bicycle bar, my little son cried 'peep,'
and, of course, I knew at once what he
meant to say, although the word had
never been used that way before.''

"What did it mean then ?'' asked Jimmieboy, interested at once.

"Why, it means 'I think he's too little to bike all by himself, papa. If his
papa looked after him as carefully as you
look after me he wouldn't let him go out
riding on that wheel without having the
hired man perched up behind to frighten
off ice carts and trolley cars !' To this I replied 'peep,' and my little boy knew that
by that I meant 'You are perfectly right,
my son, but it is very difficult to teach
human beings sense. They are not birds
and therefore have not our wisdom.' ''

"And how about 'week' and 'cheep'
and 'gurryoup'?'' asked Jimmieboy,
feeling that on the bicycle question he
had better keep quiet because his experi-
ence had been most unpleasant.   '' When

do you use them and what do they
mean?"

"Well, in a way they are like peep,
only we use them in different places.
Peep is a word for family use only—it is
what you would call a nesthold word."

"A what?" asked Jimmieboy.

"A nesthold word," replied the Robin.
"Seems to me you are getting duller all
the time."

"Well maybe I am," retorted Jimmieboy, "but I can't help it. I never heard
any such word as nesthold in my life.
We have household words, if that is what
you mean."

"You are not so dull, after all," said
the Robin kindly. "That's just what I
did mean. I thought you would see it at
once. You live in a house and the words
you use are household words. We live
in nests and, of course, the words we use
are called nesthold words. That's what
peep represents. It is for domestic use
only. Week is a word we use when we
go out into society. Take a robin party,
for instance. We all get ourselves up as
spick and span as you please, polish up
our red vests until they look like rubies,
and go to the party. As soon as we arrive
the robin that gives the party says
'week,' and we reply 'week.' That is,
she says : 'I am so glad to see you. I
was afraid perhaps you couldn't come on
account of the baby's cold. I hope it is
much better—how well he looks and
what lovely feathers he has. I do wish
my little Robby looked half as well.'
Our week is in reply, and merely signifies
that the baby's cold was nothing serious,
and we wouldn't miss the party for the
world, and isn't it splendid it cleared up

in time; that baby's feathers certainly
are becoming to him, but that her little
Robby's, though perhaps less brilliant in
color, seem to us to possess a fineness of
quality which we fear our baby's feathers
will never have. That, you see, Jimmieboy, is the meaning of week when
used on arriving at a party. A few
minutes later it will mean 'May I
have the pleasure of escorting you to
supper?' 'Yes, thanks; I think I
will go down.' 'Shall I bring you a
gnat?' I think I should prefer an ant,
thank you.' 'Certainly, it is a great
pleasure to get anything for you.' 'Oh,
dear me, how polite you are,' and so on.

PROFESSOR OF FORIEGN LANGUAGES —

It is just week, week, week all through the party. Same way at calls, or at dinners out, or at anything where we robins are on our very politest behavior. And, as we lengthen out peep sometimes with a few extra Es to make our meaning more clear, so we do with week."

"It's a wonderful language," said Jimmieboy.

"Very, and easy to learn, too," replied the Robin. "In fact, it doesn't take our baby robins a minute to learn all the conversation they need in the nest. As soon as they come out of their shells they say peep—and there you are. Then when they go out into the world they get the other words, week, cheep and gurryoup, without any difficulty."

"You haven't told me yet how cheep and gurryoup are used," said Jimmieboy.

"Cheep is our language in business," said the bird. "If Mr. Robin goes into an arrangement with a rose-bush for a supply of insects to be served at the nest every morning—just as your milkman serves you with milk—all he has to say is, cheep, and the rose-bush understands. If Mrs. Robin wishes to refit the interior of her nest with a new lot of hay or straw, all she has to do is to go to the hayfield or strawpatch and say cheep, and get all she wants.   It is simply a shopping term, like ' how much is this, ten cents a yard ? Dear me, isn't that a little high ?' or ' will you let me return this in case after I get it home I find it will not go with the carpet ?'   Cheep is a very useful word— in fact, you human beings use it a great deal in your business affairs.   ' I want something cheap,' you say.   You got that word from us.   We used it long before English was invented, and we are very glad to have you use it, but it makes us a little indignant when we learn that the makers of your dictionaries do not give us the credit for having invented it. That's one great fault I find with human beings—they pride themselves on being the only kind of living things that can talk, when as a matter of fact there was a time when we birds and animals did all

the talking and so gave you the idea of a
lot of fine words. Who gave you the
word doodle in your Yankee Doodle
song? Nobody but the rooster. Who
gave you the word cheap, as I have
already said? Nobody but the robins.
We gave you peep, too. You discovered
that as soon as we opened our eyes in the
morning we said peep, so you refer to
that time of the day as the ' peep of day,'
and when your baby wants to play you
shut your eyes, and then opening them
again cry out ' peep,' and he laughs until
his little sides ache. Who gave you the
word ' ugh?' You got that from the

pigs. You got 'bah' from the sheep. You got 'booh' from the dogs, and so on, and on you kept taking words from those you pretend to pity because they can't talk, until you had a respectable foundation on which to get up a language of your own—and we are all glad you did, because if you couldn't talk you wouldn't be happy, and we haven't lost anything by making you happy, only your dictionary people ought to acknowledge what is owed to us."

It certainly did seem as if the robin was right, and Jimmieboy had no fault to find with his claim to the recognition of his kind as the founders of spoken language. Passing the question over, however, he asked.

" And gurryoup?"

" That," said the robin, sadly, " is the one word I regret in our language. We use that when we fight. It is the only naughty word we have. It means anything from ' you're another ' to ' say that again and I'll peck your eyes out.' It's a quarrelsome word and it's hard to kill,

But I must go now, my boy. I just
heard my family calling me—hear—hear
that ?"

Jimmieboy listened, and sure enough
from a neighboring tree he heard two

small voices calling "peep-peep-pee-ee-
eep !"

"My babies want me to come home
and tell them a fairy story," said the
Robin. "So, good-bye. I'm very glad,

indeed, to have met you—in other words, week-wee-ee-eek !"'

And with a gracious little nod the robin hopped away, leaving Jimmieboy wondering whether or not human beings really had got any of their words from the birds and animals. Certainly ' cheap' and ' doodle ' did seem to prove the truth of what the robin had said, not to mention the word ' ugh,' which undoubtedly was taken from the pigs.

A Submarine Adventure.

A Submarine Adventure.

THERE was something going on in the aquarium the other evening when Jimmieboy went to say good-night to his great round-eyed gold-fish. The glittering occupant of that watery house was flopping about in the water as excitedly as if he were dressing in a hurry to catch a train to town.

"What on earth is the matter with you?" asked the boy, as he watched the busy, bustling fish for a moment. "You are jumping around just as papa does when he can't find his collar, and the carriage is waiting to take him out to dinner somewhere.''

"That's just what's the matter with me," returned the gold-fish, with a sigh of despair, "I can find my collar, but I can't find the scale to button it on, otherwise my collar-button. I'm going out to dine to-night, too, and it is getting very late. Where can I have put it? Dear me, dear me, how aggravating it all is, to be sure !''

And the poor fish hustled and bustled about, splashing the water with his tail until it spattered up over the sides of the aquarium and wet the carpet on the nursery floor.

"You mean to say that you have movable scales, do you?" asked Jimmieboy, much amazed at the idea of a fish hunting for a collar button.

"Why, of course," answered the gold-fish. "These scales are only my clothes. I can take 'em off just as you can yours whenever I want to.''

"That's funny," said Jimmieboy;

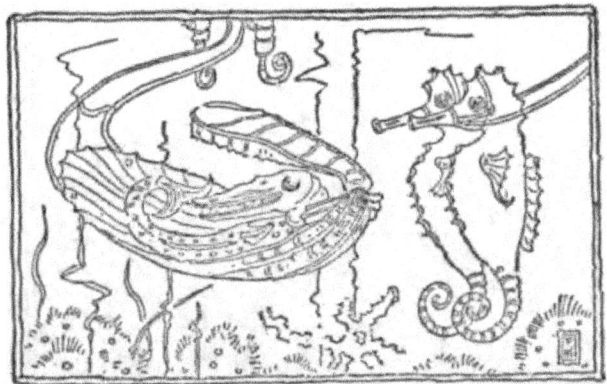

"I've never seen any of them lying around."

"Hoh!" jeered the gold-fish. "You're a great one, you are. You don't suppose that everybody's careless like you, do you? If you do, you make a great, large mistake. Just because boys strew their clothes all over the floor when they go to bed at night is no reason why fish should be so careless with their scales. Furthermore, you must remember that my scales are solid gold, and when I take 'em off I hang 'em up in a small closet I've hired in the safe deposit company. They're too valuable to leave about."

"But you lost your collar button scale just the same," said Jimmieboy. "So you needn't be so proud of yourself and so superior!"

"That isn't my fault," retorted the fish. "Collar buttons have only themselves to blame for getting lost. There is something in the collar button itself which dooms it to be lost. You ask your papa about it and he'll tell you that what I say is the exact truth. I know of a man—I used to live in an aquarium next door to his house—who once made a bet of a thousand glasses of soda water that he could keep a collar button a whole year, and another man bet him he couldn't, and they drew up a paper and had it signed by witnesses. The man who bet he could keep the button a year thought he was very smart, because instead of trying to keep it in the way the other man thought he would—in his shirt-collar—he bought a small oaken box. He put the button in the oaken box and put the oaken box in a tin box with a lock and key on it. Locking the

tin box, he put it in an inner compartment of his safe, locked the compartment
and then shut the safe door, locked that
and sent the whole thing down to the
safe deposit company.''

"He had it pretty safe, I guess," said
Jimmieboy.

"Well, he thought so," laughed the
gold-fish. "But he didn't win the bet
just the same. The bet was made at 4
o'clock in the afternoon of December 8,
1891. At 3 o'clock on the afternoon of
December 8, 1892, he went to the safe
deposit company, got the safe open,
opened the inner door, opened the tin
box, opened the oak box—"

"And it was gone?" cried Jimmieboy.

"No—keep cool," replied the fish.
"It wasn't gone at all. It was there safe
and sound. He took it out and started
off to the club to collect his bet. Five minutes of four came. He took the button out
of his pocket to show to the man he'd bet
with ; and, booh ! out it slipped from between his fingers, struck the carpet,
rolled under something—nobody knows

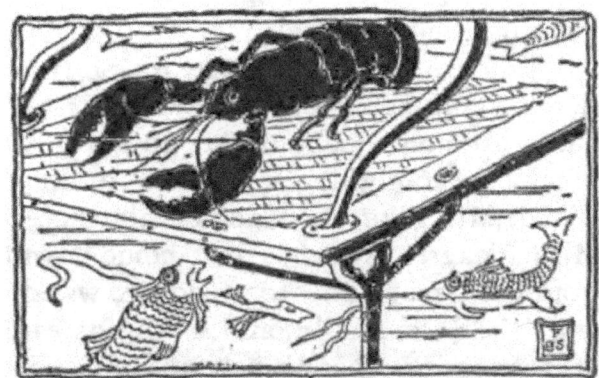

what—and hasn't been found to this day.
He'd kept the button 364 days 23 hours
and 58 minutes, but he'd slipped up on
the year by two minutes. So the other
fellow got the soda water. And it's just
that way with 'em all. There's no count-
ing on 'em at all—pshaw! And doesn't
that prove it?" the fish added, with an
angry sweep of his tail. "There it is—
right on the back of my neck, where it
ought to be, and not lost at all, with me
wasting all this time looking for it!"

Jimmieboy laughed.

"I guess what you need is somebody
to look after you," he said. "You really

ought not to go out to that dinner alone ;
you might lose yourself."

"You are right about that, possibly,"
said the gold-fish, thoughtfully. "In fact,
I'm a little scarey about this dinner I'm
going to to-night. It's given by my
friend, Mr. Pike, in honor of his niece,
Miss Pickerel, who has just come down
from the Great Lakes to spend two weeks
with the Pike family, and Pike, instead
of getting up the dinner himself, has
ordered a caterer to furnish it, and there's
something about that caterer that I don't
like. My cousin, the sunfish, went to a
dinner that this same man served once,
and he never came back."

"What became of him ?" asked Jimmieboy.

"Nobody ever knew," said the gold-
fish. "He was sitting right there at a table
eating and chatting, and all of a sudden
he gave a flip-flop and disappeared. I've
avoided these caterers' dinners ever
since."

"You'd better take me along with you,
then," said Jimmieboy. "I've been to lots

of dinners cooked by cateracts, or whatever
you call 'em, and I rather like 'em, but
they sometimes aren't so nice next morning as you'd like to have 'em. The only
headache I ever had came from a cataracts——''

"Caterer," said the gold-fish, with the
accent on the last syllable.

"Well, cater-ers, then," said Jimmieboy. "Whether they're cataracts or
caterers, I know all about 'em, and you'd
better take me along with you, because
I'll take care of you at dinner if you'll
take care of me in case of sharks."

"Needn't be afraid of them," said the
gold-fish. "They only interfere with in-
truders. If you go as my friend, the
Pikes will be glad to see you, and the
Sharks won't harm you at all. Run
along and put on your bathing suit and
come along."

So Jimmieboy did as he was told. He
put on the bathing suit, and was soon
swimming leisurely through the pipe of
the aquarium out into the sea. Just how
the pipe came to lead to the sea he never

told me, but it did, and in a short while
he and his friend, the gold-fish, stopped
at the Pikes' place, forty fathoms under
water, and about five miles out from the
New Jersey coast.

On the way out Jimmieboy was much
interested to see the huge lines of the
monster steamship Oregon that went
down near that point some years ago,
and happily enough without any loss of
life, and he was for stopping and taking
a walk on her upper deck, where he was
amused to see one or two enormous lob-
sters sitting on the steamer chairs that
still remained on board, chatting away in
a most animated fashion ; but the gold-
fish told him he'd have to postpone that
until some future time, as they were
already late for the Pike dinner.

As the gold-fish had said, both Mr. and
Mrs. Pike and all the little Pikes were
very glad to see Jimmieboy, and made
him feel quite at home. Miss Pickerel he
found charming, and as for the Sharks,
there was only one of them present, and
he was a most delightful fellow. He told

witty stories and made such fearfully
funny faces to amuse the little Pikes that
Jimmieboy was convulsed most of the
time with laughter ; and then dinner was
announced. They seated themselves about
a huge table set under the spreading
branches of a huge coral sea-weed, and all
went well until the third course, and
that third course showed the gold-fish's
wisdom in bringing Jimmieboy along to
look after him, for he was anxious to eat
it, it looked so good, and Jimmieboy
advised him not to.

"I wouldn't take any of that," said
Jimmieboy, as he read the name of the
dainty on the bill of fare. "The macaroni part of it is all right, but I don't like
the April Fool sauce that comes with
it."

"It looks awful good, though," whispered the gold-fish, his mouth watering.
"The macaroni looks like a delicious
dish of angle-worms, and I'm passionately
fond of them."

"That's all right," said Jimmieboy,
"but the April Fool sauce—"

"What's the matter with it?   What's it made of?" the gold-fish asked.

"I don't know; but I do know that April Fool food is a good thing to do without," the boy answered. "I had some caramels of that sort once, and one of 'em was stuffed with cotton and the other with red pepper."

"Will you have some of the macaroni, Goldy?" asked Mrs. Pike.

"Without the sauce, please," said Goldy, and he noticed that as he spoke the caterer glanced uneasily at him and turned pale.

"I find sauces are bad for the diges-

tion," continued the gold-fish, for he did not wish to seem to criticise his host's dinner, "and so I have given them up."

"Pass Mr. Goldy the macaroni without the sauce, then," said Mrs. Pike to the caterer. "And Mr. Jimmieboy?"

"I'll try a little, please," said Jimmieboy.

"Well, if you are going to—" began the gold-fish.

"Hush!" whispered Jimmieboy. "I only want to see what the sauce is made of."

So they all took some, with the exception of the gold-fish; and Jimmieboy, when his was placed before him, took a knife and cut it up very fine, which everybody thought was strange, but as Jimmieboy was a foreigner to them and their ways they didn't say anything. And he showed how wise he was, for just as he cut into the macaroni there came a fearful commotion in the water, and every single member of the party except Jimmieboy and his companion made a mad rush upward, even Mr. Shark.

"Wha-wha-what does it mean ?" cried the gold-fish.

"It's the April Fool Sauce," returned Jimmieboy. "See ?" And he held up his plate of macaroni, and each slender strip concealed a hook, and from each hook a scarcely visible line proceeded upward.

"They're all caught !" he moaned. "It was a mean trick—"

"Do you mean to say that that beautiful dish was—".

"So much bait !" said Jimmieboy.

"Oh dear ! oh dear !" cried the gold-fish, wringing his fins. "What baseness !"

"Yes," said Jimmieboy, sadly. "And if it hadn't been for me you'd have been caught, too !"

"But why didn't you tell 'em ?" screamed the gold-fish.

"Because my mother has told me never to criticise my food, particularly when I am dining out," sighed Jimmieboy. "What could I do after that ?"

"Nothing," said the gold-fish sadly, as

they wended their way home. "You had to obey your parents—but I wish you'd done as you usually do and forgot about it."

And Jimmieboy couldn't help wishing the same thing, too, for once—it was such a sad ending to their little adventure. He was glad, however, that his advice had saved his little friend's life; but I don't believe he ever told the gold-fish that at his next Sunday dinner he met Mr. and Mrs. Pike and Miss Pickerel again.

An Afternoon in a Hotel Room.

An Afternoon in a Hotel Room.

JIMMIEBOY had come to town for the winter and was living in a great big hotel which, while it contained no banisters on which he could slide, he liked very much because there were nineteen different kinds of dessert on the bill-of-fare every day, and buckwheat cakes always for breakfast.

"That's the way to have things," said Jimmieboy. "I like home very much, but when it comes to meals hotels are much nicer. There's always plenty more of everything downstairs, which there never is at home."

Aside from the desserts and the elevator boy, with whom he was on great terms, there was another thing about hotel life which pleased Jimmieboy very much, and that was the remarkable dial in each of the rooms by means of which anyone in these rooms could ring up anything he wanted, except the money to pay his bill—so Jimmieboy's papa had said. It was truly a wonderful thing, that dial. It had a metal needle on it which could be whirled around this way and that until the little pin at the end of it stood directly over the printed word which represented what the person who was using it wanted. On the dial itself were little divisions, and in each of these divisions was the name of some particularly nice or useful thing that anybody living in a hotel might be expected to want. For instance, turning the needle one way until it rested on the proper division, by merely pressing a button you could get a bath towel inside of two

minutes ; turning it another way and
pushing the button would bring a glass
of lemonade or a saddle-horse, according
to the division on the dial over which you
let the pin rest.   All of which seemed to
Jimmieboy to be particularly lovely, and it
was as much as he could do to keep from
experimenting with it all the time. He had
outlined in his mind a beautiful game for
stormy days, which was, briefly, to shut
his eyes, push the pointer blindly around,
press the button and then try to guess
what would come, but when he suggested
the game to his mother, she said it was
no doubt an interesting game, but that
he would better play marbles or parcheesi or something else that would not
be so disturbing to the boys in the office
who had to answer the bell.

So Jimmieboy had to content himself
with looking at the ingenious apparatus
and with imagining all sorts of fine
things that might be done with it.
One day, however, when everybody but
himself and his mother had gone out,
a card was sent up from the office stating

that a certain Mrs. So-and-so had called,
and Jimmieboy's mother, when she had
observed the state of the parlor floor,
over which marbles and parcheesi men
and paper dolls cut out of Sunday news-
papers, and other things were strewn in
great confusion, said she fancied she'd
better receive Mrs. So-and-so in the pub-
lic parlor, since it would never do to
keep her waiting down stairs for three or
four hours while she put her own parlor
in order. Hence Jimmieboy, for the first
time, was left alone in the room with the
delightful dial. He was usually an
obedient child, but until now his temp-
tation had not been very great. Here
he was all by himself with that pointer
pointing at him, and the little button
seeming to grin while it softly sung the
words, "Don't shove, just push." It
was really too much, and about ten minutes after his mother's departure Jimmieboy yielded. That little red button was
too inviting. Clambering upon a chair
which stood directly beneath the dial,
Jimmieboy seized the needle, closed his

eyes, turned it about, and pressed the button. In a minute the little bell which showed that the message had been received at the office rang, and the needle flew back.

"Dear me," cried the boy in alarm, when he realized what he had done. "I do hope it isn't a saddle-horse I've rung up."

It wasn't, for a moment later a boy knocked at the door, and in response to Jimmieboy's cheerily spoken "come in," he entered, bringing with him a half-dozen of the loveliest sardines you ever saw in your life.

"Well—that's fine !" cried Jimmieboy in delight. He'd always been fond of sardines. "It beats a grab-bag at a Sunday-school fair all to pieces."

In two minutes the sardines were eaten and Jimmieboy was back at the dial again.

"Maybe I'll get a piece of pie this time," he said.

But he didn't. This time a man in a blue flannel shirt came up and asked where the trunk was. This puzzled Jim-

mieboy. There was only one trunk in the rooms. The rest had been unpacked and sent to the store rooms, but having been asked a question, he answered it.

"In there," he said, pointing to his mother's room.

The man in the blue shirt walked in, tried the cover, and finding that it was locked—for it contained Jimmieboy's mamma's best evening dresses, and she wished to have them under lock and key—hoisted it on his shoulder and walked out.

"Where's it to go, young un?" the porter asked as he passed Jimmieboy.

"Don't know," said Jimmieboy. "I didn't know it was going anywhere."

"Maybe they'll know at the office," said the porter, and he was gone and the trunk with him.

"Funny about that piece of pie," thought Jimmieboy. "Maybe they didn't understand ; I'll try again."

Back he went to the dial and repeated his experiment.

Five minutes elapsed when up came the hall-boy again. This time, however, he didn't bring sardines, nor had he the pie which Jimmieboy had hoped for, but he did have one of the handsomest chicken salads you ever dreamed of. It looked like a beautiful garden with flowers all over it.

"Is that all?" asked the boy.

"I guess so," said Jimmieboy, his mouth watering as he gazed at the salad.

And the boy departed.

"I wish we had a chicken salad machine like you in my house," said Jimmieboy, as he gazed at the dial, meanwhile gulping down the salad as fast as he

could. " I'd give a dollar towards buy-
ing one myself."

In a little while the salad was eaten
and Jimmieboy began again at the dial.
It went on in much the same way as
before, only things began to come in more
rapidly, for Jimmieboy grew somewhat
excited as he proceeded and did not wait
for one message to be answered before
sending another. In half an hour he had
received two more plates of sardines, a
dozen postage stamps and a magnificent
bowl full of milk toast. A man came up
and built a fire, grumbling a little that he
should have to do it on a warmish day;
the electrician called and asked what was
wanted, only to be told by Jimmieboy
that he didn't know; and the sardine
boy, now grown red in the face because of his continuous trips up and
down, announced that the carriage was
ready. The bath-room had been visited
twice by the chambermaid who brought
enough bath towels to dry the Jersey
coast—or so she said—and what seemed
most singular of all, one of the waiters

appeared carrying a tray upon which stood two bottles of champagne, a glass of Apollinaris water, and a funny looking little pink drink in a glass, which looked so much like medicine that Jimmieboy did not touch it.

Finally there was a great racket in the hall, and a tremendous pounding on the door which startled poor little Jimmieboy very much.

" C—come in," he cried.

And in rushed three men with fire extinguishers on their backs, and behind them came the housekeeper, the head clerk, two porters and the proprietor of the house. The housekeeper was very pale, but she did not lose her presence of mind. Sweeping all the bric-à-brac from the mantel-piece into a large clothes basket she had the maids carry it out into the hall. The porters seized all the furniture and rushed out of the room with it ; the head clerk emptied all the bureau drawers into a sheet and had them carried out, while the proprietor grabbed up the wondering Jimmieboy and carried him down

to the office where he would be out of
the way.

Meanwhile the men with the fire extinguishers were running here and there
in the apartments looking for a fire.

"There doesn't seem to be any except
in the fireplace," said one of them, and
just then Jimmieboy's mother appeared,
bringing with her Mrs. So-and-so, who
had expressed a desire to see the rooms,
which she had been told were so attrac-
tive.

"What on earth is the matter?" cried
Jimmieboy's mother.

"Fire," said one of the chambermaids.
"We've got everything out of the room
though."

"But—where is Jimmieboy?"

"Oh, he's safe," said the housekeeper
kindly. "We had him taken down
stairs."

"He's perfectly safe, madam," said the
head clerk, "and so far as we can see so
are the rooms. The alarm seems to have
been a false one. We are very sorry this
has occurred at this time. It is very

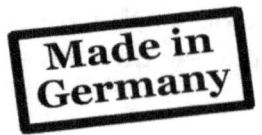

www.ingramcontent.com/pod-product-compliance
Lightning Source LLC
Chambersburg PA
CBHW060755180626
46818CB00002B/574